# OVER the HILLS & FAR AWAY

Retold and with pictures by

## CHRIS CONOVER

FARRAR STRAUS GIROUX · NEW YORK

Copyright © 2004 by Chris Conover
All rights reserved
Distributed in Canada by Douglas & McIntyre Ltd.
Color separations by Chroma Graphics PTE Ltd.
Printed and bound in the United States of America by Berryville Graphics
Designed by Barbara Grzeslo
First edition, 2004
1   3   5   7   9   10   8   6   4   2

Music arrangement and typesetting by Randa Kirshbaum,
*ran212@mindspring.com*

www.fsgkidsbooks.com

Library of Congress Cataloging-in-Publication Data
Conover, Chris.
    Over the hills and far away / Chris Conover.— 1st ed.
        p.   cm.
    Summary: A skillful piper makes everyone happy as he goes
about playing music that lightens their burdens and makes
them want to dance.
    ISBN 0-374-38043-0
    [1. Musicians—Fiction.   2. Stories in rhyme.]   I. Title.

PZ8.3.C7656Ov 2004
[E]—dc22
                                                                    2003054878

2

Tom and his pipes made such a fine squall,
His music was loved by one and by all;
The old and young, they all came out
To follow Tom and dance about.
    *Over the hills and a long way off*
    *The wind shall blow my top hat off.*

3

Tom played his pipes with such a fine skill,
That those who heard him could never keep still;
As soon as he played, they began for to dance,
Even pigs on their hooves would after him prance.
    *Over the hills and a long way off*
    *The wind shall blow my top hat off.*

4

Tom met a lad who was traveling slow,
With much to carry and far to go;
Tom took his pipes and played such a fine tune,
The poor fellow's burden was lightened full soon.
    *Over the hills and a long way off*
    *The wind shall blow my top hat off.*

5

Tom played his pipes by the river one day,
Down where the little fish swim and sway;
The fish came dancing all in a row,
Because Tom's music pleased them so.
    *Over the hills and a long way off*
    *The wind shall blow my top hat off.*

6

Tom met a maid at the market square,
And gave his heart right then and there;
He got down onto bended knee,
And said, "Sweet Molly, marry me."
    *Over the hills and a long way off*
    *The wind shall blow my top hat off.*

7

Tommy was a piper's son,
He learned to pipe when he was young;
The only song that he could play
Was over the hills and far away.

# OVER the HILLS & FAR AWAY

Tom-my_ was_ a_ pi-per's son, He learned to_ pipe_ when he was young; The on-ly_ song that_ he could play Was o-ver the hills and far a-way. O-ver the hills and a long way off The wind shall_ blow my_ top hat off.

Tommy was a piper's son,
He learned to pipe when he was young;
The only song that he could play
Was over the hills and far away.

Over the hills and a long way off
The wind shall blow my top hat off.

Tom met a maid at the market square,
And gave his heart right then and there;
He got down onto bended knee,
And said, "Sweet Molly, marry me."

Over the hills and a long way off
The wind shall blow my top hat off.

Tom played his pipes by the river one day,
Down where the little fish swim and sway;
The fish came dancing all in a row,
Because Tom's music pleased them so.

Over the hills and a long way off
The wind shall blow my top hat off.

Tom met a lad who was traveling slow,
With much to carry and far to go;
Tom took his pipes and played such a fine tune,
The poor fellow's burden was lightened full soon.

Over the hills and a long way off
The wind shall blow my top hat off.

Tom played his pipes with such a fine skill,
That those who heard him could never keep still;
As soon as he played, they began for to dance,
Even pigs on their hooves would after him prance.

Over the hills and a long way off
The wind shall blow my top hat off.

Tom and his pipes made such a fine squall,
His music was loved by one and by all;
The old and young, they all came out
To follow Tom and dance about.

Over the hills and a long way off
The wind shall blow my top hat off.

Tommy was a piper's son,
He learned to pipe when he was young;
The only song that he could play
Was over the hills and far away.

*Dedicated to my mother, Ruth Hageman Doremus*

*With great thanks to Margaret Ferguson*

*—C.C.*